WITHDRAWN

Philomel Books
an imprint of Penguin Random House LLC
375 Hudson Street
New York, NY 10014

Philomel Books is a registered trademark of Penguin Random House LLC.

Library of Congress Cataloging-in-Publication Data is available upon request.
Manufactured in China by RR Donnelley Asia Printing Solutions Ltd.
ISBN 9781524737382
1 3 5 7 9 10 8 6 4 2

Edited by Michael Green.
Design by Ellice M. Lee.
Text set in Museo.
The art was done in watercolor.

For Abe, Bella and Page—
Thanks for making every day
feel like Monday.—M.M.

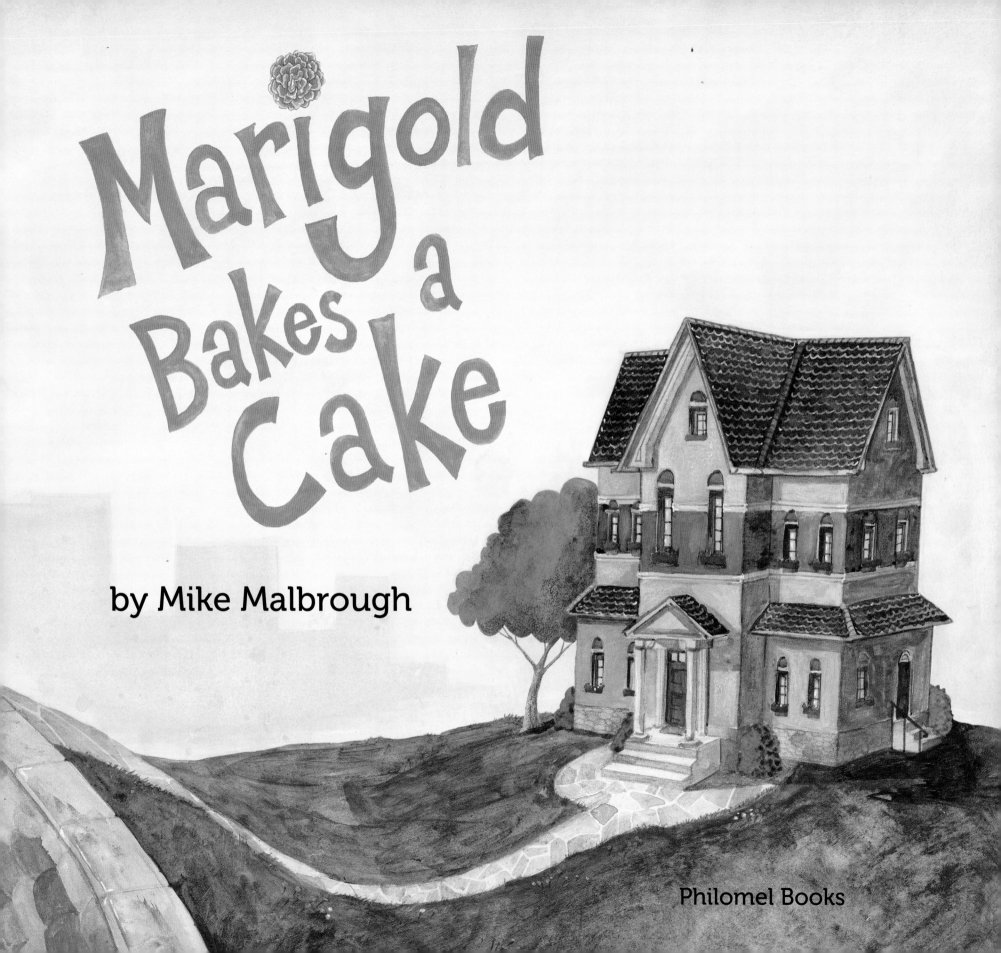

Marigold Bakes a Cake

by Mike Malbrough

Philomel Books

Marigold liked EVERYTHING just so.

His fur was always well-groomed . . .

. . . and his calendar was sorted well in advance.

Mondays were Marigold's favorite.

Because Mondays were for BAKING.

And Marigold loved to bake.

This particular Monday, Marigold wanted to
bake a cake that was absolutely, fur-sheddingly

FABULOUS.

He had plenty of ideas . . .

. . . but it had to be perfect.

With his snazziest recipes sorted, snipped and clipped for their most exquisite bits, Marigold was ready to begin.

FIRST, he separated three egg whites and whipped them up in a large mixing bowl . . .

Easy.

NEXT, he added a cup of milk . . .

Peasy.

FOLLOWED by the
juice of a lemon . . .

Squeezy.

THEN, Marigold sprinkled
in just a pinch . . .

. . . of FINCH?

"Hmm . . . that's not right," said Marigold.

"*Shoo*, Mr. Finch," Marigold said, "I've no time to chase you today. It's Monday, after all, and Mondays are for baking."

Marigold politely showed
Mr. Finch to the door.

He then returned
to his recipe, only
slightly flustered.

He *shaved* chocolate ribbons with the utmost care . . .

. . . and *drizzled* the batter with three *swirling* spoonfuls of rich molasses before tossing in just a *smidgeon* . . .

. . . of PIGEONS!

"That DEFINITELY isn't right!" said Marigold.

Marigold's tail went all poofy. A brief chase was in order.

"Skedaddle!

There is no room in my Monday for pesky pigeons!"

Marigold returned to his masterpiece a bit more frazzled than before.

Crafting buttercream pillars and fondant flowers had a calming effect. He began to hum a little tune before mixing in three tablespoons . . .

. . . of LOONS?!

"LOONS? NOOOO!"

With ears pinned back and eyes wide, Marigold leaped about the kitchen in full-on feline frenzy!

However, his tantrum
only made his guests
giggle and left his cake . . .

. . . rather less than perfect.

Marigold was full
of fuss. Perhaps a
walk would brighten
his spirits.

"Baking is for the birds," he grumbled as he shut the door.

Boy, was he wrong about that.

Baking wasn't for the birds . . .

AT
ALL.

But at least they tried.

And Marigold recognized a love of
cake-making when he saw it.

So he thought that if baking wasn't for the birds . . .
then maybe he could teach them.

He was wrong about that, too.